HONEY, WILL YOU MAKE SURE THE FRUITS AND VEGGIES ARE PUT AWAY?

SURE, MOM!

THIS IS A BORZOI BOOK PUBLISHED BY ALFRED A. KNOPF

Copyright © 2018 by Mark Hoffmann

All rights reserved. Published in the United States by Alfred A. Knopf, an imprint of Random House Children's Books, a division of Penguin Random House LLC, New York.

Knopf, Borzoi Books, and the colophon are registered trademarks of Penguin Random House LLC.

Visit us on the Web! rhcbooks.com

Educators and librarians, for a variety of teaching tools, visit us at RHTeachersLibrarians.com

Library of Congress Cataloging-in-Publication Data is available upon request.
ISBN 978-1-5247-1991-3 (trade) — ISBN 978-1-5247-1992-0 (lib. bdg.) —
ISBN 978-1-5247-1993-7 (ebook)

The text of this book was hand-lettered by the artist.

The illustrations were made using gouache with digital compositing (and a little help from a special tomato).

MANUFACTURED IN CHINA
June 2018
10 9 8 7 6 5 4 3 2 1
First Edition

FOR MY PARENTS, WHO ARE BOTH BANANAS

FRUIT BOWL

MARK HOFFMANN

Alfred A. Knopf
New York

LEAVES

PETALS

STEMS

ROOTS

IS A TOMATO A FRUIT?

WELL, THAT IS THE QUESTION OF ALL QUESTIONS. IF THE TOMATO IS NOT A FRUIT, IS HE NOT DELICIOUS? IF THE TOMATO IS NOT A FRUIT, IS HE NOT HEALTHY? DOES HE NOT HAVE JUICE LIKE YOU? YOU NEED TO LOOK INSIDE YOURSELF AND ASK WHY ANY OF US ARE FRUITS. FRUIT IS MORE THAN...

YES OR NO?